MEET ALL THESE FRIENDS IN BUZZ BOOKS:

The Animals of Farthing Wood
Thomas the Tank Engine
Biker Mice From Mars
James Bond Junior
Fireman Sam
Joshua Jones
Rupert
Babar

First published in Great Britain 1994 by Buzz Books,
an imprint of Reed Children's Books
Michelin House, 81 Fulham Road, London SW3 6RB
and Auckland, Melbourne, Singapore and Toronto

ISBN 1 85591 379 8

Printed in Italy by Olivotto

RUPERT™
and the
SNOWMEN

Story by Norman Redfern
Illustrations by SPJ Design

It was a spring afternoon. Mrs Bear was
going to have tea with her friends in
Nutwood. She put on her coat and picked
up a hat.

  "It's funny," she told Rupert. "I can't find
my red hat anywhere. I shall just have to
wear my brown one instead."

She said goodbye to Rupert, and set off down the path to Nutwood.

Rupert knew that he had seen the red hat somewhere, but he couldn't remember where. He began to search for it. In the hall cupboard, amongst the coats and umbrellas, he found a cardboard box. Perhaps the hat was inside it.

He put the box on the kitchen table, lifted off the lid and peeked inside. But instead of his mother's hat, he found a dozen brand new Christmas crackers. He was about to shut the box again when a strange noise made him jump.

Tap! Tap! Tap! Someone was knocking at the window.

"Who's there?" he called.

"It's me," said a voice. "Jack Frost."

"Hello, Jack," said Rupert, opening the window. "Come and see what I've found."

"Crackers!" cried Jack when he saw the box. "But it's not Christmas!"

"My mummy gave them to me to take to Bill Badger's Christmas party," replied Rupert. "But Bill was ill, and he didn't have a party, after all."

"Poor old Bill!" said Jack.

"What are you doing in Nutwood, Jack?" asked Rupert. "We're not expecting snow today, are we?"

"I've lost one of my father's snowmen," said Jack sadly.

It was Jack Frost's job to collect all of the snowmen at the end of winter. When everyone in Nutwood was fast asleep, Jack would blow his whistle, and a strong wind would whisk the snowmen back to King Frost's palace in the far frozen North.

"My father has been checking my lists,"
said Jack. "And he says that one of the
Nutwood snowmen is missing."

"Oh, no!" cried Rupert.

"And when I searched the palace, I found
an extra snowman who shouldn't be
there," Jack said. "Oh Rupert, what can
I do?"

"I know," said Rupert. "Take me back to
the palace with you. I'll help you look for
the missing snowman!"

Jack Frost led Rupert out of the cottage
and into the garden. Then he gave a shrill
blast on his whistle.

"Hold tight," he said. "We're off to the
frozen North!"

Suddenly, a gust of wind swept Rupert and Jack off their feet. It carried them into the air, high above Nutwood. On and on, over the clouds they flew, until at last they fell slowly back towards the ground.

"Look!" cried Rupert. "The Ice Palace!"

14

King Frost's great palace was dripping
with icicles. Rupert shivered as he landed
on the snowy path outside the door.

"Follow me!" said Jack.

He led Rupert down a long, dark passage.
At the end was a tall door, which creaked
when Jack opened it.

"Sssh!" said Jack. "I don't want my father to hear us."

Together they tiptoed into the hall.

"Look!" whispered Jack.

Rupert gasped. The Great Hall was full of snowmen. Some wore hats and woolly scarves, and they all had smiling faces. Jack pulled out his notebook and showed Rupert the list of Nutwood snowmen.

16

"They're listed by house," he said. "That one with the purple scarf is from Algy Pug's garden. The one with the earmuffs..."

"He came from my garden!" cried Rupert.

"Yes," said Jack, "but you see, there's one snowman on the list who just can't be found. Look — no hat or scarf, last seen in Bill Badger's garden. And now," he said tearfully — "I've lost him!"

Rupert looked very thoughtful.

"I remember that Bill wanted to give his snowman a smart outfit," he said. "But on Christmas Eve, he started feeling ill. His mummy sent him up to bed before he could put on his snowman's hat. When did you make your list, Jack?"

"Christmas Day," replied Jack.

"You see," Rupert went on. "I went to
see Bill on Boxing Day. When I saw his
snowman without a hat, I went home and
borrowed one of my mummy's. It was a red
one, with a big red bow. I'd forgotten all
about it!"

19

"So!" cried Jack, "my list is wrong. Bill's snowman was wearing a hat after all!"

"Where is the extra snowman, Jack?" asked Rupert excitedly.

Jack showed him a smiling snowman wearing a smart red hat.

"That's Bill's snowman!" Rupert cried. "He's wearing my mummy's red hat!"

"Well done, Rupert!" said Jack, happily.
"Now I must tell my father."

"Tell me what, Jack?" asked a voice. King
Frost was standing in the doorway. He was
usually a cheerful soul, but today he was
frowning. "Are you going to tell me how
you lost one of my snowmen?" he said.

"I can explain that," said Rupert.

He told the King all about Bill's snowman, and his mother's red hat.

"So, now we've found your lost snowman and my mummy's lost hat," said Rupert.

"And my list was right, after all," said Jack cheerfully.

King Frost didn't say a word. He strode across the hall and spoke in a low voice to the snowman with the red hat. Rupert wasn't sure, but he thought he saw the snowman nodding. Then, the King took Rupert's mother's hat off the snowman's head, and brought it back to Rupert.

"We've decided," said King Frost, "that the best solution is to give you back your hat, Rupert. Now we can tick off the snowman without the red hat, as it says on the list."

He took Jack's notebook and made a tick.

"Well done, Jack," he said, smiling. "And Rupert, thank you for your help."

24

"Phew," sighed Jack, as King Frost swept out of the Great Hall. "I'm glad you remembered about that red hat, Rupert!"

"So am I," said Rupert. "Now, I'd better go back to Nutwood before my mummy comes home. She'll be pleased to have her hat back."

Jack led Rupert back outside the palace.

"When I blow my whistle, the wind will carry you home again," he said. "Are you ready?"

"Just a minute, Jack," said Rupert. "May I ask you a favour?"

"Of course you may," said Jack.

Back in Nutwood, Rupert put the red hat on the kitchen table, next to the box of Christmas crackers. Shortly, he heard his mother coming up the garden path.

"Hello, Rupert," she said. "My red hat! You've found it! But why are these crackers on the table?"

"I was wondering," said Rupert, "if we could have a special party for Bill, since he missed his Christmas party."

"What a good idea," said Mrs Bear.

"May we have mince pies, and a chocolate log?" asked Rupert.

"You'll be asking for snow next," laughed Mrs Bear.

"I already have," thought Rupert. "I hope Jack remembers!"